LBRockStars
LizaBaker
PattiAnnHarris
LizCasal

NAT

lauren hodge

I AM FOREVER THANKFUL!
<u>YOU</u> MADE BIRDIE HAPPEN!!!

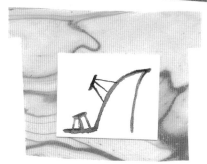

EMILY
SCOTT

NO SHOE CLOSET COULD EVER BE BIG ENOUGH
TO LIST ALL THOSE I AM SO GRATEFUL FOR. YOU
KNOW WHO YOU ARE . . . THANK YOU XO!

LAURA
SANTISI

From the bottom of my bare feet, thank you:

Mom, for putting me in big-girl shoes . . .
John, for helping me around in them . . .
and Bob, for sweeping me off them every day.

stored in a database or retrieval system, without the prior written permission of the publisher. • Little, Brown Books for Young Readers • Hachette Book Group • 237 Park Avenue, New York, NY 10017 • Visit our Web site at www.lb-kids.com •
Little, Brown Books for Young Readers is a division of Hachette Book Group, Inc. • The Little, Brown name and logo are trademarks of Hachette Book Group, Inc • First Edition: September 2009 • Library of Congress Cataloging-in-Publication
Data • Rim, Sujean. • Birdie's big-girl shoes / by Sujean Rim.—1st ed. • p. cm. • Summary: Five-year-old Birdie loves her mother's shoes, but when she is finally granted permission to wear some for a little while, she discovers that her "barefoot
shoes" are best of all. • ISBN 978-0-316-04470-7 • [1. Shoes—Fiction. 2. Play—Fiction. 3. Mothers and daughters—Fiction.] • I. Title. • PZ7.S33232Bir 2009 • [E—dc22] • 2008043799 • 10 9 8 7 6 5 4 3 2 1 • IM • Printed in China •
The illustrations for this book were done in watercolor and collage on watercolor paper. • The text and display type were set in Horley Old Style. • Book design by Liz Casal

BIRDIE'S BIG-GIRL SHOES

SUJEAN RIM

LITTLE, BROWN AND COMPANY
Books for Young Readers
New York   Boston

Whenever Birdie's mother got ready in the morning, Birdie was there to help.

She would start by picking out the sparkly jewelry.

Next she would find the perfect pair of sunglasses.

Then her dog, Monster, would help her choose just the right perfume.

LA CREAM

But more than anything in the whole wide world,
Birdie longed to wear her mother's shoes.

She loved her crocodile pumps
and her summer peep-toes
and all her strappy sandals. . . .

Birdie couldn't wait a minute longer.

"Mommy, I think I'm ready to wear big-girl shoes."

Monster wasn't so sure.

"Birdie, you'll have years and years to wear
high heels," her mother said. "I promise."

Birdie imagined how grown up she'd feel dancing in high heels.

She thought about how much better she would be at hide-and-seek. Monster would never find her.

She pictured how fun it would be to cartwheel
in beautiful shoes, her feet glittering in mid-air.

"Mommy?" Birdie asked again later,
"could I wear your shoes, just for a little while?"

        "Oh, Birdie," her mother said.

"I promise to be careful, cross my heart!
Pretty please?"

Birdie's mother looked into
her daughter's hopeful eyes.

"Well . . . okay, sweetheart.
But you have to be very careful."

"I will, I will, **I will!**" she promised,
then raced to her mother's shoe closet.

Birdie carefully slipped her
little toes into one shoe,
then slid into the other.

She looked at herself in the mirror . . .
and gasped.

She felt *beautiful.*

She felt *glamorous.*

. . . She felt like a *movie star.*

"Let's shim-sham, Monster!"
said Birdie as she started to dance.

But twisting wasn't easy in
wobbly peep-toes.

"Let's play hide-and-seek, instead.
I'll hide first!" she decided.

But hiding was impossible with
pointy Mary Janes
sticking out.

"Cartwheel time!" Birdie shouted.

But landing sure was tricky in sky-high stilettos.

Barefoot, Birdie
did the best cartwheels
she'd ever done.

She tangoed

and hand-spun

. . . then she kicked off the other.

First she kicked off one shoe . . .

Birdie looked down.

Her feet were sore and her
knees were scraped.

This is no fun, Birdie thought.

She knew just what
she needed to do.

and grand-jetéd all across the living room.

At bedtime, she played hide-and-seek.

Her mother couldn't find her.

"Here I am!"

From that day on,
Birdie decided she
wasn't quite ready for
grown-up shoes—yet.

For now, she liked her
beautiful barefoot shoes
most of all.

D O N

J. LOURA

SAB

LIBBY **K.**

john m & jennifer

eleanor

MIN